Night House
Bright House

Monica Wellington

DUTTON CHILDREN'S BOOKS • NEW YORK

Night House
Bright House

Monica Wellington

DUTTON CHILDREN'S BOOKS · NEW YORK

For my parents and my sister, Laura,
and my daughter, Lydia

With special thanks to Andrew Kupfer, Barbara Lagow,
and Kelly Kynion, and always, Lucia Monfried

Library of Congress Cataloging-in-Publication Data
Wellington, Monica.
Night house, bright house / by Monica Wellington. — 1st ed.
p.   cm.
Summary: During the night, all the objects in the house
wake up and cause an uproar.
ISBN 0-525-45491-8
Special Markets ISBN 978-0-525-42618-9 Not for resale
[1. Night—Fiction. 2. Stories in rhyme.] I. Title.
PZ8.3.W4595Ni 1997 [E]—dc20 96-24550 CIP AC

Published in the United States 1997 by Dutton Children's Books,
a division of Penguin Books USA Inc.
375 Hudson Street, New York, New York 10014
Designed by Amy Berniker and Sara Reynolds
Manufactured in China
2 4 6 8 10 9 7 5 3

Gouache, watercolors, and colored pencils were
used to create the full-color art for this book.

This Imagination Library edition is published by Penguin Group (USA), a Pearson
company, exclusively for Dolly Parton's Imagination Library, a not-for-profit
program designed to inspire a love of reading and learning, sponsored in part by The
Dollywood Foundation. Penguin's trade editions of this work are available wherever
books are sold.

"Time to get up,"

said the  cup.

Waking, Shaking in the Studio

"Shh—it's night," said the 🛋 light.

"Pit-a-pat," said the 🪆 mat.

"Chug-chug," said the 🏺 jug.

"Jingle-jangle," said the ⭕ bangle.

"Clinkety-clank," said the 🐷 bank.

"Loop-de-loop," said the ⭕ hoop.

"You're bad," said the 📝 pad.

"GO," said the 🎀 bow.

Sneaking, Peeking in the Bedroom

"What's that noise?" said the toys.

"Quiet down," said the crown.

"We need to sleep," said the sheep.

"Yakety-yak," said the sack.

"Gobbledygook," said the book.

"Doodle-de-doo," said the shoe.

"What an uproar," said the door.

"Move on," said the swan.

Helter, Skelter Down the Stairs

"Here they come," said the drum.

"Higgledy-pop," said the mop.

"Dickory-dock," said the clock.

"Fiddle-dee-dee," said the key.

"Ziggity-zag," said the bag.

"Scoot," said the boot.

"Scat," said the hat.

"Now scram," said the pram.

Racing, Chasing
to the Kitchen

"Get ready," said the spaghetti.

"Here they are," said the jar.

"What a clutter," said the Butter butter.

"Don't get flustered," said the mustard mustard.

"Look out, please," said the cheese.

"Tickle-tickle," said the pickle.

"Phony-baloney," said the macaroni.

"Run," said the bun.

Dashing, Splashing in the Bathroom

"Rub-a-dub," said the tub.

"Drippity-drip," said the ship.

"What a mess," said the dress.

"They'll clean up," said the cup.

"You think?" said the sink.

"Let's hope," said the soap.

"Fat chance," said the pants.

"Lots of luck," said the duck.

Giggling, Wiggling in the Living Room

"Crash, boom!" said the  broom.

"Oh NO," said the domino.

"Don't look," said the book.

"I'm fainting," said the painting.

"Did something break?" said the snake.

"You bet," said the TV set.

"Boo-hoo," said the statue.

"Spells trouble," said the bubble.

Telephone Book
Yellow Pages

Twirling, Whirling in the Front Hall

"Slow down," said the 🤡 clown.

"For my sake," said the 🍰 cake.

"How exhausting," said the 🎂 frosting.

"Just crazy," said the 🌼 daisy.

"Super-silly," said the 🌸 lily.

"Leave things alone," said the ☎ phone.

"You're telling me," said the 🔑 key.

"Stay cool," said the 💎 jewel.

Bumping, Jumping
in the Dining Room

"Surprise!" said the 🥧 pies.

"This is great," said the 🍽️ plate.

"First-class," said the 🥛 glass.

"Just dandy," said the 🍬 candy.

"A dream," said the 🍨 ice cream.

"I'm tired out," said the 🫖 spout.

"I agree," said the ☕ tea.

"Enough's enough," said the 🧁 cream puff.

Pattering, Clattering in the Back Hall

"Just stop," said the top.

"It's late," said the skate.

"I suppose," said the rose.

"Poppycock," said the block.

"We're done in," said the pin.

"Get upstairs," said the bears.

"It's about time," said the chime.

"That's what I think," said the ink.

Back in the Bedroom, Snuggling, Cuddling

"Hush," said the brush.

"Pipe down," said the crown.

"Curl up," said the cup.

"Snug as a bug," said the rug.

"Close your eyes," said the ties.

"Sweet dreams, mice," said the dice.

"Sleep tight," said the kite.

"Love you," said the shoe.

"That's all,"

said the  ball.